# THE DAY THE RABBI DISAPPEARED
## *Jewish Holiday Tales of Magic*

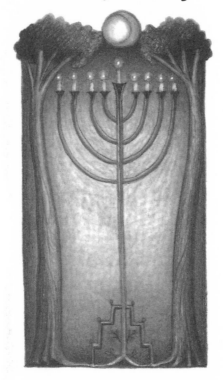

retold by Howard Schwartz
illustrated by Monique Passicot

The Jewish Publication Society
Philadelphia
2003    5763

For Shira
Nathan and Miriam

and for Tsila
with thanks
—H. S.

For Miau Miau
—M. P.

ACKNOWLEDGMENTS

Some of these stories have previously appeared in *Cricket*, the *Learn Torah With* series, *Judaism*, *Spider*, and *Tikkun*.

Special thanks to my editor, Deborah Brodie, who guided this book from its inception.

Thanks, too, to Arielle North Olson, Marc Bregman, and Vered Hankin for assistance in the editing of these stories.

Thanks also to Yocheved Herschlag Muffs, Judaica consultant, and to Janet B. Pascal, copy editor.

"Drawing the Wind" was written in collaboration with Arielle North Olson.

A recording of some of the stories in this book by storyteller Vered Hankin is available. For more information, please contact veredstory@hotmail.com.

First paperback edition 2003.  All rights reserved
ISBN: 0-8276-0757-1

This edition is reprinted by arrangement with Viking Children's Books, a member of Penguin Putnam, Inc.

The Jewish Publication Society
2100 Arch Street, 2nd floor
Philadelphia, PA  19103

Manufactured in the United States of America

03 04 05 06 07 08 09 10  10 9 8 7 6 5 4 3 2 1

# CONTENTS

## INTRODUCTION

The story is told of a king who was about to sign an evil decree against the Jews. The people were terrified, but Rabbi Elimelech insisted they go ahead and celebrate the Sabbath as always. He said the Sabbath blessings. Then, before anyone began the meal, Rabbi Elimelech swept his arm across the table and knocked over a bowl of soup.

Later it was learned that at that very moment, just as the king was going to sign the decree, he accidentally knocked over the inkwell, spilling ink all over the parchment. The king took it as an omen. He tore up that evil decree and ordered that none like it should ever be drawn up again.

This tale recounts how a wise rabbi was able to save the Jewish community through magic. From a historical point of view, the story may well be a legend. But in the nineteenth century, people regarded it as a true account of a great sage who was famous for his magical powers.

The kind of magic Rabbi Elimelech uses in this story is known as sympathetic magic. Using it, a person can directly affect something that happens elsewhere, even at a great distance. This is only one of many kinds of magic found in this collection of tales.

Note that in the story, Rabbi Elimelech proceeds with the ritual of the Sabbath despite the danger. The Jewish people believe they are closest to God during the holy days—including the Sabbath—and it is essential, from the Jewish point of view, to maintain this close contact with the Divine. Indeed, during the most important of these holidays, Rosh Hashanah and Yom Kippur, a person's life is said to hang in the balance, as the decision is made in Heaven whether the person's name will be inscribed and sealed in the Book of Life.

Sometimes these tales of magic are linked with specific Jewish holidays. In this collection, one tale has been included for each of ten important holidays, as well as for Rosh Hodesh and the Sabbath. The first story is linked to Rosh Hodesh, the first day of the month, and the last story is linked to the Sabbath, the last day of the week. Readers wanting to know more about these holidays will find information following the stories.

Holidays serve an important role in these stories. Every holiday is a time of heightened awareness and closeness to God, but as these stories attest, they could be times of great danger as well. Then rabbis take on the role of sorcerers and come to the rescue, as did Rabbi Elimelech in the tale of the bowl of soup.

Indeed, Rabbi Elimelech, who came from the city of Lizensk in Poland, was one of a long line of Jewish sorcerers going all the way back to Moses. When Moses held his staff over the Red Sea (also known as the Sea of Reeds), the waters of the sea parted (Exodus 14:21). So, too, when Moses struck a rock with his staff, water came forth (Numbers 20:11). It is not hard for us to look at that staff as a kind of magic wand, and the parting of the sea as a kind of magic. But in this case, of course, the source of the magic is God.

Perhaps the greatest Jewish sorcerer of all was King Solomon, who knew the languages of the birds and even of the winds. He had a magic ring with God's name on it, which gave him unlimited powers, and a magic carpet that took him wherever he wanted to go.

King Solomon served as the model for all Jewish sorcerers who came after him. Among them were Rabbi Adam, who once moved a palace hundreds of miles in the blink of an eye, and Rabbi Judah Loew, who created the Golem, the man made of clay, which he brought to life by pronouncing God's secret name.

Jewish tradition holds that there is a secret pronunciation of God's four-letter name, YHVH. It is said that there is only one great sage in every generation who knows how to truly pronounce this name, and whoever knows this secret has unlimited powers at their command. Indeed, Jews do not pronounce God's name when it appears in prayers, out of concern that someone might accidentally pronounce God's name in the right way, and who knows what would happen then? Instead, they say *Adonai* (God) or *Ha-Shem* (the Name).

But God is not the only name with magic powers. There also are secret names of angels that, when pronounced, are the keys to magical feats. Indeed, angels are often found in these magical stories. Four angels give Rabbi Hanina ben Dosa a ride to Jerusalem, along with a beautiful stone he brings as a gift to the Temple. And Rabbi Hayim Pinto calls upon Rahab, the Angel of the Sea, to recover a treasure lost in a shipwreck.

So, too, are there remarkable tales about heavenly journeys, where rabbis ascend on high to study the secrets of Jewish mysticism. And there are mysterious figures who appear and serve as guides in times of great danger, such as the old man in "The Cottage of Candles" who watches over everyone's soul candle until it goes out and the soul takes leave of this world.

Another mysterious figure appears in "The Enchanted Menorah." Here the Baal Shem Tov dreams about Mattathias, the father of the Maccabees, who lived two thousand years ago, only to awake and find Mattathias waiting to guide him home in a blizzard. Dreams, in fact, are among the primary ways that God communicates with people in these stories. In "The Angel of Dreams," Rabbi Or Shraga asks a dream question before he goes to sleep. When the Angel of Dreams can't reach the rabbi, his wife receives the dream instead.

Still another kind of magic is used by Rabbi Nachman of Bratslav in "The Souls of Trees." After waking from a nightmare, he uses the mystical technique of opening a holy book at random and pointing to a passage, which serves not only to interpret his dream, but also to explain why the innkeeper and his wife have remained barren.

Yet even though these rabbis function as sorcerers, they know well that the complete source of their power comes from God, and from their unshakable faith in God. And even though they have great powers, their aim is not to accomplish supernatural effects for their own benefit, but only to promote the well-being of the Jewish people. Indeed, from this perspective, what occurs in these stories is not so much magic as miracles of God. This is the essence of Jewish magic, for ultimately the Jewish people depend on God and not on magic to guard and protect them.

# A FLOCK OF ANGELS
## *A Rosh Hodesh Tale*

Long ago, in the Kurdish town of Mosul, there lived a young woman named Asenath who was known for performing wonders. Her blessings were often sought by women who wished to have babies, or by sick people who wished to be cured. Her touch had healing powers, especially for children.

Asenath had learned everything from her father, Rabbi Samuel Barzani, who was well acquainted with the secrets of Heaven. He had taught these secrets to her until her wisdom and powers were as great as his own. It was whispered among the people that the spirit of her father rested upon her, and for this reason she was known as Rabbi Asenath.

After Rabbi Samuel died, he often came to his daughter in dreams. He would reveal dangers to her and tell her how to ward them off, saving many lives. One night Asenath dreamed that Rabbi Samuel told her to go to the Kurdish town of Amadiyah for Rosh Hodesh, the celebration of the new moon. He told her that the Jews of Amadiyah needed her protection.

When it became known that Rabbi Asenath was planning to travel to Amadiyah, the people of her town pleaded with her not to go, for things had become dangerous for the Jews living there. "All Jews have been warned to stay away from Amadiyah," they warned her. "If you go, you will surely be risking your life!" But Asenath had made up her mind. She bid farewell to the people of her town and began her journey.

When Rabbi Asenath reached the town that she had visited so often, she was given great respect as a holy woman. But the people were upset when she told them that they should celebrate Rosh Hodesh outdoors, so they could see the crescent of the new moon, as was their custom. They wanted to stay in the safety of the synagogue, for they knew they were surrounded by enemies and that their very lives were in danger. "Don't be afraid," she told them. And their faith in God and their trust in her were so great that they agreed to proceed as in the past, despite the danger.

So on the night of Rosh Hodesh, all the people came out to celebrate the new moon and the new month. At first they were cautious, yet soon they were singing and dancing in the town square with abandon. But suddenly there were shouts and they saw flames shoot up into the sky. The synagogue had been set on fire! Thank God, no one had been inside it. Yet they could not bear to see their synagogue consumed in flames. Many men had to be held back so they wouldn't run inside and be burned to death while trying to save the Torah scrolls. Everywhere people wept, falling to their knees, for they knew the flames were fast approaching the Ark where the Torahs were kept.

At that very moment, Rabbi Asenath whispered a secret name, one that she had learned from her father. All at once the people heard a loud flapping and a great wind swirled around them, and they thought that a flock of birds must be overhead. But when they looked up, they saw a flock of angels descending to the roof of the synagogue. The angels beat the flames with their wings, until every last spark had been put out. Then they rose up into the heavens like a flock of white doves and were gone.

The people were awestruck. They cried out, "Angels! Angels!" And when the smoke cleared, they saw that another miracle had taken place: the synagogue had not burned. Nor was a single letter of any of the Torahs touched by the flames.

When the enemies of the Jews learned of the miracle of the angels and saw how the synagogue had been saved from the fire, they were so fearful that they dared not harm the hair of even a single Jew.

As for the Jews of that town, they wept and prayed and thanked God for saving them and their beloved synagogue. And they were so grateful to Rabbi Asenath that they renamed the synagogue after her, and it is still standing to this day.

And all this came to pass because of Rabbi Asenath's courage and loyalty in honoring her father's wish, conveyed in a dream, that she go to that town for the celebration of the new moon.

*Kurdistan, seventeenth century*

ABOUT

"A FLOCK OF ANGELS"

*Rosh Hodesh*

Rosh Hodesh marks the beginning of a new Jewish month. The new month begins when the new moon appears. In Biblical times, months were calculated by the moon, and Rosh Hodesh was a minor festival. Special offerings were made, and the shofar, the ram's horn, was sounded, as written in Psalms 81:4: *Sound the shofar on the new moon . . . for the festive day.* In talmudic times, the beginning of a new month was declared when two witnesses saw the crescent of a new moon and reported it to the Sanhedrin, the high court. They relayed this information by lighting signal fires on hilltops.

Jewish legend records that God made Rosh Hodesh a special day for women, to reward them for refusing to help their husbands build the golden calf at Mount Sinai. It was traditional for women not to work on this day. In recent years, Jewish women have rediscovered Rosh Hodesh as a time to celebrate the rebirth and renewal of women and the moon. They also choose Rosh Hodesh for a naming ceremony for baby daughters or as a time to meet for religious and educational purposes.

### Rabbi Asenath Barzani

Until the modern era, very few women were given the title of "Rabbi." But sometimes a woman's wisdom and learning were so exceptional that this title was given to her. Such is the case with Rabbi Asenath Barzani, who lived in Mosul, Kurdistan, from 1590 to 1670. Another instance was Hannah Rochel Werbermacher, known as the Maid of Ludomir, who lived in Eastern Europe in the nineteenth century and was also recognized as a rabbi. Rabbi Asenath was the daughter of Rabbi Samuel Barzani, who headed many yeshivas (schools for Jewish students) during his lifetime, and whose authority in Kurdistan was absolute. He was a master of Kabbalah, the Jewish mystical tradition, and he was said to have taught many of its secrets to his daughter.

After Rabbi Barzani died, many Jews made pilgrimages to his grave in Amadiyah. His daughter adored her father, whom she regarded as a king of Israel. He was her primary teacher, and after his death she took over many of his duties. Not only did Asenath serve as a rabbi, but she became the head of the Yeshivah of Mosul, and eventually became known as the chief teacher of Torah in Kurdistan. In addition, she was a poet and an expert on Jewish literature, and there are many Kurdish legends about the miracles she performed, such as the one described in "A Flock of Angels."

## DRAWING THE WIND
### *A Rosh Hashanah Tale*

Long ago, on the Spanish island of Majorca, a young boy spent most of each day at the shore, sketching the ships that sailed into the harbor. Solomon was a wonderful artist, everyone agreed. His drawings seemed so real that people wondered if the waves in his pictures were as wet as they seemed—or the sun as hot.

His father was a great rabbi who really preferred Solomon to spend his time studying, but Solomon would always slip away to the shore.

A few days before Rosh Hashanah, the Jewish New Year, a ship arrived from the city of Barcelona. Solomon overheard one of the sailors talking to a local merchant.

"There's news from Spain that will make every Jew on this island tremble."

"What is it?" asked the merchant.

"The king and queen have decreed that all the Jews in the land must give up their religion and become Christian."

"And if they refuse?"

"Then they must leave at once," said the sailor.

"But what if they want to stay?"

"Then they lose their lives."

Solomon was frightened. He didn't want to leave his beautiful island. He ran home to tell the news to his father, Rabbi Simeon ben Tsemah Duran.

"Must we leave, Father?" asked Solomon.

"I cannot leave, my son," said his father. "The other Jews look to me for guidance. I must stay until they all escape. But you should go, and I will join you later in Algiers."

"I won't leave you," said Solomon. "You are all I have since Mother died. Surely God will protect us."

Rabbi Simeon hugged his brave son. "Then let us work together and spread the word that everyone must meet in the synagogue." They hurried through the village, knocking at the doors of every Jewish home and shop.

When everyone had gathered at the house of prayer, Rabbi Simeon told them about the terrible decree.

"Save us!" they cried out in fear.

They hoped their beloved rabbi would work a miracle. For they knew his prayers had once turned back a plague of locusts. Another time, when crops were withering in the fields, his prayers had brought rain.

"You have only three choices," Rabbi Simeon told the men. "You can escape by sailing to Algiers. You can stay and pretend to convert, but secretly remain a Jew. Or you can defy the king and queen. As for me, I would rather go to my grave than say that I am giving up my religion." Solomon realized how strong his father was and how Rabbi Simeon strengthened and comforted his people.

In the days that followed, most of the Jews crowded onto ships, carrying very little with them. They saw to it that the women and children took the first available ships. Some Jews stayed and pretended to convert, in order to save their lives. They were known as *Conversos,* but in secret they continued to follow their Jewish ways.

Only a handful of Jews openly refused to convert. Among them were Solomon's father and Solomon himself. They planned to leave together, once they were certain that all those who wished to escape had done so.

By then it was the start of Rosh Hashanah. Rabbi Simeon and Solomon and those few who dared to enter the synagogue prayed with great intensity that year, in hope that their names would be written in the Book of Life. For Rosh Hashanah is when that decision is said to be made. Surely God would hear their prayers and guard them.

All went well the first day, but on the second day of Rosh Hashanah, just after the sounding of the shofar, soldiers rushed into the synagogue and dragged them all away. They were cast into a prison cell, where Rabbi Simeon continued to lead the prayers for Rosh Hashanah by heart. Solomon would have been terrified if he hadn't seen how calm his father remained.

None of them slept that night. Even though Rosh Hashanah had ended, they stayed awake, praying. The cell was very dark, with only one high window. But at dawn it let a little sunlight in. When Rabbi Simeon saw it, he said, "Have faith, my brothers. For just as there is a bit of light, so there is hope, and I feel that God has heard our prayers and will protect us."

The guard overheard them and laughed. "You think you have hope? You have just three days to live. Then you die. Let's see what your God does for you then."

Rabbi Simeon saw how frightened they were. So he turned to Solomon and said, "Won't you help us pass the time? Why don't you draw one of those ships you do so well?"

Solomon couldn't believe his ears. His father was asking him to draw? Solomon felt in his pocket and pulled out his last piece of chalk. When he looked up, he thought he saw a hint of a smile on his father's face.

Solomon remembered all the ships he had watched from the shore, and he began to draw the one he thought was the most beautiful on the sunlit wall. He drew the wind that filled the great sails, and he added barrels of wine and bushels of wheat.

Solomon's father and the other men watched him draw until the sun set and the prison cell was enveloped in darkness. Then they began to pray to God to save them. Once again, they prayed all night long.

The next day, Solomon continued to work on his drawing. Little by little he finished every detail of the ship, and then he drew the sea around it. The waves looked as if they might spill right off the wall and splash onto the floor.

The picture seemed finished, but Solomon didn't want to stop. His father suggested that he draw the two of them, there on the deck. This Solomon did, and all the men marveled at the fine resemblances he drew. Then the second day in

prison ended, and again they prayed throughout the night.

When the sun rose on the third day, one of the men asked Solomon to draw him on the ship, too. "For I would like to be with you." And one by one, the others made the same request. But when darkness fell, Solomon had not finished drawing the last man.

That night they prayed to God with all their hearts, for they knew the execution was set for sunrise the next day. All of the men shook with fear, except for Rabbi Simeon. Solomon took strength from his father, and he, too, remained unafraid.

As soon as the first light of dawn came through the window, Solomon took out his chalk and quickly finished drawing the last man.

Just as he drew the final line, he heard keys jangling. The soldiers were coming to unlock the door to their cell. Then Solomon and all the men would be taken to the courtyard for their execution.

Solomon turned to his father and saw that he was deep in prayer. And, at that very moment, he heard his father pronounce God's secret name out loud.

Suddenly Solomon could not hear the guards in the hallway, and when he looked down, he saw that he was standing on the deck of the beautiful ship he had drawn on the prison wall.

His father and all the other men in the picture were with him, safely aboard a real ship floating on a real sea. The sails strained against the wind, just as they had in Solomon's drawing, and the ship sped away from danger.

All the Jews from the prison cell rejoiced with Solomon and his father—for they knew they were aboard a ship of miracles, on their way to freedom. They would never forget that Rosh Hashanah, the Day of Judgment, when God had seen fit to save them.

*The Balkans, oral tradition*

ABOUT
"DRAWING THE WIND"

*Rosh Hashanah*

Rosh Hashanah, the Jewish New Year, takes place on the first day of the Hebrew month of Tishre (in September or October). Traditionally, it represents the birthday of the world. It starts a ten-day period known as the Days of Awe, which concludes on Yom Kippur, the Day of Atonement. Starting on Rosh Hashanah, Jews examine their lives, to see if they are living up to their own ideals and those of their religion. It is also a time for making amends to those who have not been treated fairly, so that the new year can be started with a clean slate.

It is believed that on Rosh Hashanah a decision is made in heaven whether or not a person will live another year. That is why it is known as the Day of Judgment. Although this decision is made on Rosh Hashanah, it is not sealed until Yom Kippur, ten days later. It is possible, during this period, to reverse the decree by repentance, prayer, and acts of charity. That is why it is said that "the gates of repentance are always open" (Deuteronomy Rabah 2:12 and Lamentations Rabah 3:15). On Rosh Hashanah the shofar is sounded in the synagogue, and it is considered an obligation for all Jews to be present to hear it.

*The Expulsion*

In 1492, King Ferdinand and Queen Isabella signed a decree expelling all Jews from Spain. Jews who did not convert to Christianity or leave were sentenced to death. This decree included people living on the Spanish island of Majorca. Hundreds of thousands of Jews were expelled from

Spain and went into exile in many countries, especially in the lands of the Middle East. Of those Jews who remained, many pretended to convert, but secretly carried out Jewish rituals. These people are known as *Conversos* or *Marranos*. If they were caught in the broad net of the Spanish Inquisition, they were tortured and executed. Thousands of Jews lost their lives. Even so, many persisted in remaining secret Jews. To this day there are Catholic Spaniards who practice certain Jewish rituals, such as the Sabbath blessing over bread and wine, although they no longer remember why. They are descended from those *Conversos*.

### Rabbi Shimon ben Tsemah Duran

Rabbi Simeon (Shimon) ben Tsemah Duran, the leader of the Jewish community of Majorca in the fourteenth and fifteenth centuries, was highly respected as a rabbinic scholar. He also was a physician and surgeon with a vast knowledge of mathematics, astronomy, and science.

Although Rabbi Simeon was born in 1361 and died in 1444, before the Expulsion took place in 1492, he was such a towering presence that legend has placed him in Majorca during the Inquisition that followed, as in this tale. In reality, Rabbi Simeon and his family left Majorca for Algiers after a massacre that took place in 1391. There, Rabbi Simeon continued to be recognized as one of the great leaders of his time.

### The Tetragrammaton

The secret name of God that Rabbi Simeon pronounces in this story is known as the Tetragrammaton. It was believed that whoever knew how to pronounce this name had great powers. King Solomon is said to have used the power of the Name to capture Ashmodai, the king of demons. And Rabbi Judah Loew of Prague is said to have used it to bring to life the Golem, a man made of clay. According to Jewish tradition, only one great sage in each generation knows the secret pronunciation.

## The Cottage of Candles
### *A Yom Kippur Tale*

There once was a Jew who went out into the world to seek justice. He saw how people mistreated each other, and how hard they were on the animals. Surely, he thought, the world was not that harsh everywhere. Somewhere, he was certain, true justice must exist, but he had never found it. So he set out on a quest that consumed most of his years. He went from town to town and village to village searching for justice. But never did he find it.

In this way many years passed, until the man had explored all of the known world except for one last, great forest. He entered that dark forest without hesitation, for by now he was fearless. He went into the caves of thieves, but they mocked him and said, "Do you expect to find justice here?" And he went into the huts of witches, but they laughed and said, "Do you expect to find justice here?"

Now, it happened that the man lost track of time in his wanderings. At sunset on the eve of Yom Kippur, the Day of Atonement, he arrived at a little clay hut that looked like it was about to collapse. Through the window he could see many flickering flames, and he wondered why they were burning. He knocked on the door, but there was no answer. As he waited, he noticed that the whole forest had grown silent. Not a single bird sang. He knocked again. Nothing. At last he pushed the door open and stepped inside.

As soon as he entered that cottage, the man realized that it was much larger on the inside than it had seemed to be from the outside. He saw that it was filled with hundreds of shelves, and on every shelf there were dozens of oil candles. Some of those candles were in precious holders of gold or silver or marble, and some were in cheap holders of clay or tin. Some of the holders were filled with oil and the flames burned brightly. But others had very little oil left, and it seemed that they were about to sputter out.

All at once an old man stood before him. He had a long, white beard and was wearing a white robe. "*Shalom aleichem,* peace be with you, my son," the old man said. "How can I help you?" The man who sought justice replied, "*Aleichem shalom,* with you be peace. I have gone everywhere searching for justice, but never have I seen anything like this. Tell me, what are all these candles?"

"Each of these candles is the candle of a person's soul," said the old man. "As long as that person remains alive, the candle continues to burn. But when that person's soul takes leave of this world, the candle burns out."

"Can you show me the candle of my soul?" asked the man who sought justice. "Follow me," the old man said, and he led the way through that labyrinth of a cottage, which appeared to be endless. At last they reached a low shelf, and there the old man pointed to a candle in a holder of clay. The wick of that candle was very short, and there was very little oil left. The old man said, "That is the candle of your soul."

Now, the man took one look at that flickering candle, and a great fear fell upon him. Was it possible for the end to be so near without his knowing it? Then he happened to notice the candleholder next to his own. It was full of oil, and its wick was long and straight and its flame burned brightly. "And whose candle is that?" the man asked.

"I can only reveal each man's candle to himself alone," the old man said, and he turned and left.

The man stood there, staring at his candle, which looked as if it was about to burn out. All at once he heard a sputtering sound, and when he looked up, he saw a wisp of smoke rising from another shelf, and he knew that somewhere, someone was no longer among the living. He looked back at his own candle and saw that there were only a few drops of oil left. Then he turned to the candleholder next to his own, so full of oil, and a terrible thought entered his mind.

He stepped back and searched for the old man, but he didn't see him anywhere. So he lifted that oil candle, ready to pour it into his own. But all at once the old man appeared out of nowhere and gripped his arm with a grip like iron. And the old man said: "Is this the kind of justice you are seeking?"

The man closed his eyes. And when he opened his eyes, he saw that the old man was gone, and the cottage and all the candles had disappeared. He found himself standing alone in the forest and heard the trees whispering his fate. He wondered, had his candle burned out? Was he, too, no longer among the living?

*Afghanistan, oral tradition*

ABOUT
## "THE COTTAGE OF CANDLES"

### Yom Kippur

Yom Kippur, which takes place on the tenth of the Hebrew month of Tishre (in September or October), is the Day of Atonement, the holiest day of the Jewish year. Jews the world over mark it by praying and fasting, soul-searching and repenting, seeking God's forgiveness. For twenty-five hours all Jews, except for those who are too young or too ill, take no food or water. On Yom Kippur, a person's life is said to hang in the balance: will his or her name be sealed in the Book of Life for the year to come? It is a day to reconcile with God and with anyone we may have wronged in the preceding year. Yom Kippur is sometimes called "the Sabbath of Sabbaths," because it is such a special day. Like the Sabbath and all other holy days, it begins at sunset the night before and ends the next evening, at sunset. The prayers and melodies of Yom Kippur are especially beautiful and moving, and the whole service and experience of Yom Kippur can be exceptionally profound. At the end of Yom Kippur the shofar is sounded, and those who have spent the day in fasting and prayer come away with the hope that their names are inscribed and sealed in the Book of Life.

### The Sources of This Story

"The Cottage of Candles" is a perfect example of a folktale based on Biblical verses. Consider the following: *Justice, justice shalt thou pursue* (Deuteronomy 16:20) and *The soul of man is the candle of God* (Proverbs 20:27). Note how the first verse sets in motion the quest that propels the story, and how the second is the focus of the climactic episode about the cottage of candles. This story was told in the harsh land of Afghanistan, where justice is still hard to find. It is not difficult to imagine how the Biblical verses that serve as the foundation of this tale inspired it, for surely the longing for justice in a place like Afghanistan could easily lead to such a tale.

Behind almost every Jewish tale, there is some Biblical concept or episode or verse. For example, the next story, "Four Who Entered Paradise," alludes to the journey of Elijah into Paradise in a fiery chariot at the end of his life (2 Kings 2:11), while the story told in the Bible in the Book of Esther hangs over everything that happens in "The Angel of Dreams."

### The Keeper of the Soul Candles

The identity of the old man in this story remains a mystery. The Keeper of the Soul Candles functions as an Elijah-like figure who is hidden in the forest. Perhaps he is one of the *Lamed-Vav Tzaddikim*, the thirty-six hidden saints who are said to serve as the pillars of the world. God is said to sustain the world because of their presence. Or he might be viewed as the Angel of Death. Perhaps he is even God. The fact that the story takes place at Yom Kippur suggests that the old man might well be God, who judges the man who seeks justice on the Day of Judgment.

### Divine Tests

Many of the most important stories in the Bible are divine tests, such as that of Adam and Eve and the forbidden fruit, or the binding of Isaac, or the suffering of Job. "The Cottage of Candles" is another example of such a divine test. The man seeking justice attempts to fulfill the Biblical injunction *Justice, justice shalt thou pursue* by setting out on a quest to find justice.

Such quests are quite common in Jewish tales and in general folklore, too, although they are rarely this abstract. Usually, they are a quest for something such as a golden bird, a lost princess, or the sword of Moses. Each quest tests the character of the individual involved. Instead of proving worthy, the man who seeks justice attempts to lengthen his life at the expense of someone else's, but he is caught and pays the price. In this sense he does find justice, for justice is exactly meted out.

### The Jewish Idea of Justice

The concept of justice as found in the American Declaration of Independence is directly linked to the Jewish ideal, as stated in the verse *Justice, justice shalt thou pursue.* This pursuit of justice serves as the model not only for democratic nations, but for the peoples of nations living under dictatorships, who long for the day when they will find justice as well. In this context, "The Cottage of Candles" might be seen as a folk meditation on the idea of justice. The moral of the story is clear: Those who seek justice need to search for it not only out in the world but also inside themselves.

## FOUR WHO ENTERED PARADISE
### *A Sukkot Tale*

On the seventh and last night of Sukkot in the Moroccan town of Azmor, it was the custom to stay up until dawn, studying the mysteries of the Torah without interruption. It is said that the gates of heaven open for an instant during this night, and any wish made at this time will be fulfilled.

So it was that the leading sages of the city—Rabbi Shimon, Rabbi Reuven, and Rabbi Moshe—had gathered in Rabbi Yakov's sukkah, a booth covered with leaves, to study the very secrets of Jewish mysticism, known as Kabbalah.

Now, Rabbi Shimon had a daughter whose name was Yona, who accompanied her father to Rabbi Yakov's house. Yona was curious about what her father and the others were doing in the sukkah. So, late at night, when no one noticed, she left the house and peered inside. There she saw her father and the others deep in study. She watched them for a while and then returned to the house.

A little later Yona came back to the sukkah and looked inside again. This time the sukkah was empty. Yona could not understand where her father and the others had gone. Then she happened to glance at a silver plate hung in the sukkah, and in it she saw four pairs of eyes, which she recognized as those of her father and his friends!

Yona was terrified. How could they have disappeared? Where had they gone? And what was the meaning of the eyes she saw reflected in that silver plate? She could not stop trembling. She was about to run back into the house to tell the oth-

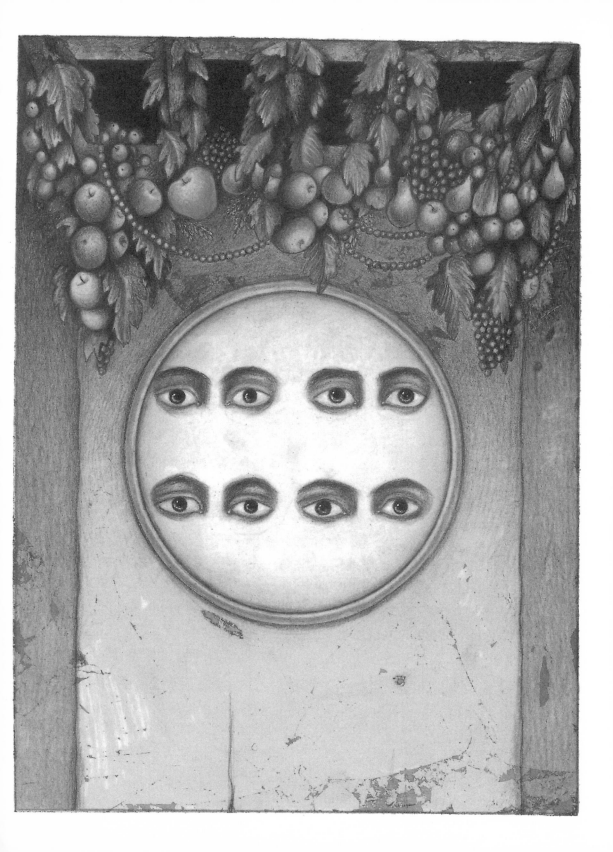

ers what had happened when suddenly the four rabbis appeared in the sukkah once more, and their eyes were no longer reflected in the plate.

Yona could not restrain herself and ran into the sukkah, crying. She embraced her father and clung tightly to him. Then she told him what she had seen and asked him what it meant. Rabbi Shimon replied: "Yona, I am very sorry you were so frightened. You see, we were studying the mysteries of Kabbalah when, all at once, the heavens parted, and an angel invited us to study Kabbalah in heaven. But because we are not allowed to look upon God, we left our eyes behind when we ascended on high. That is what you saw."

*Morocco, oral tradition*

ABOUT

## "FOUR WHO ENTERED PARADISE"

### Sukkot

Sukkot begins on the fifteenth of the Hebrew month of Tishre (in September or October) and ends seven days later. The seventh and final day of Sukkot, when this story takes place, is known as Hoshanah Rabbah. It is customary to stay up studying all night on Hoshanah Rabbah. In particular, the Zohar and other books of a mystical nature are read at that time, as happens in this story.

Sukkot is one of the three Jewish pilgrimage festivals, along with Passover and Shavuot. In ancient times, before the Temple in Jerusalem was destroyed, Jews in the land of Israel would try to make pilgrimages to Jerusalem on these days to bring harvest offerings to the Temple. Of these three festivals, Sukkot most retains the character of a harvest festival. The *lulav*, a palm branch, and the *etrog*, a citron fruit, are carried during Sukkot services. During the seven days of Sukkot, some Jews eat and sleep in booths known as *sukkot* that are erected beside their homes or synagogues, or on rooftops of apartment buildings, with only leafy boughs serving for the roof. This is to remind them of the wandering of the Israelites in the wilderness during the time of the Exodus, when the people had to live in temporary dwellings.

There is a kabbalistic tradition that the three Jewish patriarchs, Abraham, Isaac, and Jacob, together with Joseph, Moses, Aaron, and David, come to visit the sukkah on each night of the holiday. One of them is specifically welcomed on each of the seven nights. There is a new custom of also inviting the four matriarchs, Sarah, Rebekah, Rachel, and Leah, along with Miriam, Deborah, and Esther, or other female leaders, to visit in the sukkah.

### The Four Who Entered Paradise

It is often possible to find the models for Jewish folk stories in earlier sources. Hasidic tales are often based on kabbalistic ones, and kabbalistic tales find their model in rabbinic tales, and at the bedrock of Jewish tradition is the Torah, from which almost all Jewish stories are ultimately drawn. The original heavenly journey was that of Elijah found in the Bible, where *a fiery chariot with fiery horses suddenly appeared . . . and Elijah went up to heaven in a whirlwind* (2 Kings 2:11).

This account was drawn upon by an ancient tale from the Talmud about four sages who entered Paradise. After they returned, Ben Zoma is said to have lost his mind, Elisha ben Abuyah to have lost his faith, and Ben Azzai to have lost his very life. Only Rabbi Akiba survived. This legend is a very mysterious one, and there are many opinions about what it means.

But it is clear that the story included here, "Four Who Entered

Paradise," which was collected in modern-day Israel, finds its source in the Talmudic model, although here all four rabbis ascend and descend in peace. The reason for their success may be that they learned from the errors of the ancient sages. In the Talmud it says that "Ben Azzai looked and died." Because it is forbidden to look directly at God, the four Moroccan rabbis avoided this danger by leaving their eyes behind; and in this way their lives were saved. Thus we see how a theme first found in the Bible is still being echoed in a tale collected orally in Israel during the last forty years.

### Jewish Mysticism

Mystics long to have direct knowledge of God. Since Jews believe that God is in Heaven, they sought to find a way to travel to Heaven, so they could be closer to God. The four rabbis in this Moroccan story find the opportunity to go to Heaven on Sukkot, when the sky opens for an instant, and an angel invites them to study Kabbalah—Jewish mysticism—in Paradise. The fact that the four were invited to make this journey means their greatness had been recognized in Heaven, and that is why they were able to make such a blessed journey.

### Rabbi Shimon Elkayam

Rabbi Shimon Elkayam, known as Rabbi Shimon the Hazan, since he was a cantor, served as a rabbi in the Moroccan town of Azmor from 1930 to 1949. As a child, he studied Torah in the city of Marrakesh. When he was twenty, he went back to Azmor and studied Torah with the rabbis of that city. Rabbi Shimon also studied Kabbalah and wrote twelve books, though none were published, and only one manuscript remains, in the hands of his son in Jerusalem. The other three sages who appear in the story are Rabbi Reuven Kohen, Rabbi Moshe Kohen, and Rabbi Yakov Rawami.

## THE FLYING SHOE
### *A Simhat Torah Tale*

Every year the followers of the Baal Shem Tov, known as Hasidim, celebrated Simhat Torah with wild dancing and singing. That is the joyous day when the reading of the Torah is begun anew, and Jews dance with the Torah in their arms.

Then one year his Hasidim noticed that the Baal Shem Tov did not join in the dancing, but stood off by himself. He seemed to be strangely somber on that joyful day. Suddenly a shoe flew off the foot of Rabbi Dov Baer as he whirled in the dance, and at that instant the Baal Shem Tov smiled.

A little later the Hasidim saw the Baal Shem Tov pull a handful of leaves out of his pocket, crush them, and scatter their powder in the air, filling the room with a wonderful scent, like that of Paradise. Then the Baal Shem Tov joined in the dancing with great abandon. The Hasidim had never seen him so happy, and they, too, felt possessed by a greater joy than ever before.

Afterward, when they had all caught their breath, one of the Hasidim asked the Baal Shem Tov what he had smiled about, after having been so solemn.

The Baal Shem Tov replied: "While you were dancing, I went into a trance, and my soul leaped from here into the Garden of Eden. I went there to bring back leaves from the Garden, so that I could scatter them among us, making this the happiest Simhat Torah of all time. I gathered fallen leaves with the greatest pleasure and put them in my pocket. As I did, I noticed that there were scattered fringes of prayer shawls in the Garden, as well as pieces of worn tefillin, from the straps Jews wrap

around their arm when they pray. Not only that, but I saw heels and soles and shoelaces, and sometimes even whole shoes. And all of these objects were glowing like so many sparks—even the shoes—for as soon as they entered the Garden of Eden, they began to glow.

"Now I was not surprised to see the fringes and straps, for they come from sacred objects, but I wondered what the shoes were doing there.

"Just then a shoe flew into the Garden of Eden, and I recognized it at once as that of Rabbi Dov Baer." The Baal Shem Tov turned to face him. "Dov, I realized that your love of God was so great that your shoe had flown all the way there. That is when I understood why there were shoes in the Garden of Eden. And that is why I smiled.

"I would have come back to join you at that very moment, but just then I saw two angels in the Garden. They had come to sweep and clean the Garden and to gather those precious, glowing objects.

"I asked the angels what they were going to do with the shoes, and one of them said: 'These shoes have flown here from the feet of Jews dancing with the Torah. They are very precious to God, and soon the angel Gabriel will make a crown out of them for God to wear on His Throne of Glory.'"

The Baal Shem Tov stopped speaking, and all who heard this story that day were filled with awe. Nor was Rabbi Dov Baer's shoe ever seen again, for it had truly flown to the Garden of Eden.

*Eastern Europe, eighteenth century*

ABOUT

## "THE FLYING SHOE"

### Simhat Torah

Simhat Torah follows the seventh day of Sukkot and is a day of rejoicing. On Simhat Torah, the year-long reading of the Torah comes to an end with the last few verses of the Book of Deuteronomy and starts again with the first verses of the Book of Genesis. The scrolls of the Torah are taken from the Ark and carried around the synagogue in a procession that makes seven circuits around the sanctuary. After each circuit, there is singing and dancing with the scrolls. It is a celebration of great joy for having lived to complete the reading of the Torah for another year. In some Hasidic circles, there is wild dancing, as in this tale.

### The Baal Shem Tov

Rabbi Israel ben Eliezer, known as the Baal Shem Tov, "Master of the Good Name," was the founder of Hasidism. He was born in approximately 1700 and died in 1760. There are hundreds of miraculous legends about him, but very few facts about his life are known. He is said to have been an orphan who spent most of his time in the fields and forests and later served as a teacher's assistant. He studied Jewish texts on his own, but he kept his knowledge hidden until the age of thirty-six. Then he became known as a healer and *baal shem*, a miracle worker.

The Baal Shem Tov made his home in the Polish town of Medzhibozh, where he attracted many followers, known as Hasidim. This movement grew into a major spiritual revival in Judaism. The Baal Shem Tov emphasized the importance of *kavanah,* or intensity, in prayer, and dancing and singing as a way to come closer to God. His teachings also involved a revival of attention to Kabbalistic texts. His followers included Rabbi Dov Baer, who became his successor. The next story in this collection, "The Enchanted Menorah," is also about the Baal Shem Tov.

## The Garden of Eden

The Garden of Eden *(Gan Eden)* represents Paradise on earth. It is first introduced in the book of Genesis, in the story of Adam and Eve. Adam and Eve were expelled from the Garden of Eden when they disobeyed God's command not to eat the fruit of the Tree of Knowledge. God then placed an angel with a flaming sword to guard the entrance of the Garden of Eden. Although the gates of the Garden were closed after this, there are quite a few visits to the Garden recounted in Jewish folklore, such as that of the Baal Shem Tov in this story. This shows how Jewish folktales draw on Biblical themes and retell them, perpetuating the influence of the Bible in Jewish tradition. Today the Garden of Eden symbolizes the idea of perfection, where there is harmony between nature and people.

## THE ENCHANTED MENORAH
### *A Hanukkah Tale*

A long time ago, before Rabbi Israel ben Eliezer became known as the Baal Shem Tov, he and his wife Hannah lived in the Carpathian Mountains. During the week, Rabbi Israel wandered by himself in the dense forests there. He loved nature and studied everything he saw, the deer and fawn, the birds and squirrels, and all the animals that were in the forest.

All week, during all kinds of weather, in summer or winter, he would walk alone and meditate among the trees. And on Friday, just before sundown, he would return home for the Sabbath.

During the week in which Hanukkah was to be celebrated, Rabbi Israel told his wife, "With God's help, I will return home on the eve of Hanukkah to light the first candle. But if I am late for some reason and haven't arrived before sundown, don't wait for me, but light the candle by yourself and put the Hanukkah menorah in the window."

On the afternoon of the eve of Hanukkah, just as Rabbi Israel was about to return home, it started to snow, and a strong wind arose. Soon a blizzard was raging. Rabbi Israel buttoned up his coat, leaned on his heavy staff, and tried to make his way through the storm. Darkness was falling, and for the first time in his life, Rabbi Israel was lost. He could not find the narrow path in the forest that led to his home.

He walked and walked but somehow always returned to the same place. Yet because of his trust in God, he did not lose faith. He was only upset that he would not be able to light the candles on the first night of Hanukkah.

Soon Rabbi Israel became exhausted. He sat down to rest on a large stone, and because he was so tired, he fell asleep. While he slept, an image appeared in his dream of a tall old man carrying a candle in his hand. "Who are you?" the sleeping rabbi asked. The old man replied, "I am Mattathias, the father of the Maccabees, and I have brought this candle for you." At that instant Rabbi Israel awoke, and he was able to make out the dim shape of a person walking before him through the swirling snow. That person held a menorah in his hand, with one candle burning, a menorah that looked very much like Rabbi Israel's own.

Rabbi Israel picked up his staff and started following the light of the flame. For what seemed hours, he never let it out of his sight. At last he saw that he was not far from the place where he walked on the Sabbath. As he came closer, he recognized the fields and trees and saw that he was approaching his own village. Then he saw his own house. And there was his Hanukkah menorah in the window, its first candle lit with a clear and bright flame.

Rabbi Israel's wife stood outside the house, wrapped in her heavy winter shawl, deeply worried about him. It was already past midnight, and she was afraid that something had happened to him in that terrible storm.

When Rabbi Israel appeared on the path, she ran to him and embraced him. "Thank God that you have come home alive!" she said. There were tears of happiness in her eyes. "When it was becoming dark," she said, "and you hadn't returned, I lit the first candle of Hanukkah by myself. But no sooner did I light it than the candle and menorah vanished from the window. I was terrified, for I was sure it must be a sign that you were in danger."

Then Rabbi Israel understood that Mattathias had taken the menorah from his window and used it to guide him back home. He told his wife about his dream, and about the silent figure who had guided him through the forest. Before they entered the house, he pointed to the window and she saw that the menorah had been restored to its place. The flame of the candle glowed brightly in the night.

*Germany, oral tradition*

ABOUT
## "THE ENCHANTED MENORAH"

### *Hanukkah*

Hanukkah, which begins on the twenty-fifth day of the Hebrew month of Kislev (in December), marks the victory of Judah Maccabee and his followers over the Syrian army in the second century B.C.E. The victory of the Maccabees preserved Judaism. Thus the story of Hanukkah is the struggle of the Jewish people to remain Jewish. After their victory, the Temple in Jerusalem, which the Syrians had defiled, was rededicated. A legend in the Talmud reports that a miracle took place. Although there was not enough oil to keep the Temple menorah lit for the eight days it would take to make new oil, nevertheless the oil lasted that long. For this reason, Hanukkah has become known as the "Festival of Lights."

To celebrate the victory, an eight-day festival was created. It is observed by lighting a candle on the first night of Hanukkah and adding an additional candle each night. These candles are held in a special Hanukkah menorah, called an *hanukkiyah,* the kind of menorah found in this story.

## THE SOULS OF TREES
### *A Tu bi-Shevat Tale*

One day Rabbi Nachman of Bratslav told his Hasidim to ask Lepke the coachman to prepare for a journey. When the Hasidim wondered where he was going, all Rabbi Nachman said was "We are needed somewhere."

Soon the coachman arrived, and Rabbi Nachman invited three of his Hasidim to join him. Then, just as they were about to depart, Lepke asked Rabbi Nachman where he wanted to go. Rabbi Nachman replied, "Hold the reins loosely, Reb Lepke, and let the horses go wherever they please." The coachman was surprised, but he did as the rabbi asked.

The Hasidim rode for many hours, while the horses took one road after another, proceeding as if they knew exactly where they were going. When the sun began to set, the Hasidim wondered where they would spend the night. At last one of them asked Rabbi Nachman, and all he replied was "God will provide."

Then, just as darkness was falling, the carriage reached an inn. Rabbi Nachman called out for the coachman to stop, and everyone got out.

The Hasidim had never been to this inn before, so they were delighted to find that it was run by a Jew and his wife. But before long they noticed that the innkeeper seemed to be very sad, though they dared not ask him what was wrong.

Now the innkeeper had heard of Rabbi Nachman and treated him with great respect and consideration. He and several other Jews who were staying at the inn joined Rabbi Nachman and the Hasidim for evening prayers. All together there were ten men, just enough to make a *minyan*. After the innkeeper's wife served a fine meal, the innkeeper showed the Hasidim to their rooms. But before he left Rabbi Nachman, he asked if he could discuss something with him in private.

"Surely," said Rabbi Nachman, and he offered the innkeeper a chair. When the man was seated, he told Rabbi Nachman his story: "My wife and I have been married for ten years, and we love each other deeply. But there is one sadness that fills our lives and overshadows everything else. For there is nothing in the world that we long for more than a child of our own. But so far God has not blessed us with a son or daughter. Rabbi, is there anything you can do to help us?"

Rabbi Nachman was silent for a long time. Then he said: "It is late and I am tired. Let me get a good night's sleep, and in the morning I will see if there is anything I can do for you." The innkeeper was pleased with this reply and took his leave of Rabbi Nachman.

Soon Rabbi Nachman and all the Hasidim were sound asleep. But in the middle of the night, Rabbi Nachman began to cry out loudly, waking up everyone in the inn. They came running to see what had happened.

When he awoke, Rabbi Nachman ignored all those who had gathered in his room wanting to know what was wrong. Instead, he picked up a book, closed his eyes, opened the book at random, and pointed to a passage. And there it was written, "Cutting down a tree before its time is like killing a soul."

Rabbi Nachman assured all those who had gathered there that he had recovered from his fright, and everyone could go back to sleep. "Let us rest," said Rabbi Nachman, "and in the morning we will speak." Everyone went back to sleep, except for the innkeeper and his wife, for they longed to know what the rabbi would tell them.

After morning prayers, Rabbi Nachman turned to the couple and asked them if the walls of that inn had been built out of saplings that were cut down before their time. The innkeeper and his wife looked at each other, and then back at Rabbi Nachman. "Yes," said the innkeeper, "it is true. But how did you know?"

Rabbi Nachman took a deep breath and replied: "All night I dreamed I was surrounded by the bodies of those who had been slain. I was very frightened. Now I

know that it was the souls of the trees that cried out to me. And now, too, I know why you have remained childless."

"Rabbi," sighed the innkeeper, "I do not understand. What do the saplings have to do with our not having children?"

"You see," said Rabbi Nachman, "there is an angel called Lailah, the angel of conception. She is the one who delivers the soul of the unborn child. But each time Lailah approaches your inn to bring you the blessing of a child, she is driven back by the cries of the souls of the trees that were cut down before their time."

"Oh, Rabbi, that is terrible," said the innkeeper. "Is there anything we can do?"

"Yes," said Rabbi Nachman. "You must plant trees all around this inn—twice as many trees as were cut down to build it. You must let them grow and take care that none of them are cut down. After three years, if the new trees have remained untouched, you will be blessed with a child."

The couple was overjoyed to hear this. That very day, even before Rabbi Nachman and his Hasidim took their leave, they began planting.

All the trees that the couple planted grew tall and strong. And after three years, Lailah returned to their home. The lullaby of the living trees quieted the cries of the trees that had been cut down, so that Lailah was able to reach the couple's house, tap on their window, and bless them with a child.

Lailah came back to the couple's home six more times. And every year that she did, the innkeeper's wife gave birth, until they were the parents of seven children, all of whom grew straight and tall as fine trees.

*Eastern Europe, nineteenth century*

ABOUT
## "THE SOULS OF TREES"

### Tu bi-Shevat

Tu bi-Shevat, which takes place on the fifteenth day of Shevat (in January or February), is the New Year for Trees. This holiday celebrates God and God's creations. On this day it is customary to eat foods from Israel that grow on trees, especially almonds and the fruit of carob trees. Some people celebrate by holding a Tu bi-Shevat Seder. This ritual was created in the sixteenth century by Kabbalists living in Safed in Israel.

In modern Israel, Tu bi-Shevat is a time for planting trees. Planting trees was considered so important by the rabbis that Rabbi Yohanan ben Zakkai taught, "If you are planting a tree and you see the Messiah coming . . . finish planting the tree and then go greet the Messiah." Folk tradition holds that, on Tu bi-Shevat, trees lean over and kiss each other. Almond trees, which are the first trees to blossom in Israel, are the ones most closely associated with Tu bi-shevat. Although this story, "The Souls of Trees," does not take place on Tu bi-shevat, it emphasizes both the sacred quality of trees as living beings and the importance of planting them.

### The Sacredness of Trees

This story suggests that trees, like human beings, have souls, and therefore they must be treated with care and consideration. It is interesting to note that the Bible also compares people to trees, as in the passage *For*

*Man is the tree of the field* (Deuteronomy 20:19). In the Psalms, a person's life is again directly compared to that of a tree: *And he shall be like a tree planted by the rivers of water, that brings forth fruit in its season* (Psalms 1:3). In fact, there is such great respect for trees that the Torah itself is compared to a tree: *It is a tree of life to those who cling to it* (Proverbs 3:18). According to Jewish law, newly planted trees and any fruits they produce are to be left alone for three years, until it is clear that the tree is strong enough to survive.

### Rabbi Nachman of Bratslav

Rabbi Nachman of Bratslav was one of the most important Hasidic rabbis. He was the great-grandson of the Baal Shem Tov, the founder of Hasidism, and is widely considered to be the greatest Jewish storyteller of all time. During his lifetime in the late eighteenth century, he had a small but devoted circle of followers, known as the Bratslav Hasidim, who believed that he had great wisdom and trusted him entirely to guide their lives. Rabbi Nachman used many methods to teach his Hasidim, including the telling of stories. He was not only sensitive to humans but also to the presence of spirits and, as we see in this story, even to the souls of trees.

Before his death, Rabbi Nachman told his followers that they would not need to appoint a new rabbi after he died, for he would always be their rabbi. They followed his instructions, although it was a Hasidic custom to appoint a new rabbi when the old one died. Even to this day, the Bratslav Hasidim are thriving in Israel and the United States, and they still follow the teachings of Rabbi Nachman.

### Jewish Divination

Divination seeks to look into the future in order to decide a matter of importance. The Bible clearly states that any kind of divination is forbidden: *There shall not be found among you any one who makes his son or daughter to pass through the fire, one who uses divination, a soothsayer, or an enchanter, or a sorcerer, or a charmer, or one who consults a ghost or familiar spirit, or a necromancer. For whosoever does these things is an abomination unto the Lord* (Deuteronomy 18:10–12).

Nevertheless, various methods of divination were practiced by the Jewish people. Even in the Bible, King Saul goes to the Witch of Endor and has her call up the ghost of the prophet Samuel, so that Saul might ask him a question (I Samuel 28). It is also believed that the High Priest in the Temple in Jerusalem used the precious gems on his breastplate to perform divination.

In this story, Rabbi Nachman seeks the meaning of his dream by opening a book at random and pointing to a passage. This is a method of Jewish divination known as *she'elat sefer*. The book most commonly used for this kind of divination is the Bible, but the book that Rabbi Nachman consults refers to a passage from the Talmud: *Cutting down a tree before its time is like killing a soul.* This gives him the essential clue to link his nightmare with the suffering of trees.

Although various kinds of oracles were popular in the past, modern Jews rarely use any kind of divination.

# The Angel of Dreams
## *A Purim Tale*

For two years, the city of Yezd in the land of Persia was besieged by rebels opposed to the Shah. Everyone in the city was in danger. Just before the holiday of Purim, the rebels gained the upper hand, and it looked as if the city were about to fall. In desperation, the Shah called upon Rabbi Or Shraga and implored him to pray for the city. The Shah had always been good to the Jews, and Rabbi Shraga promised to do so.

That night Rabbi Or Shraga asked a dream question, hoping that heaven would reveal how he could protect the city from falling into the hands of the enemy. The rabbi slept deeply that night, but when he awoke in the morning, he could not remember a single dream. He was terribly disappointed. He had been certain that Heaven would send him a dream in reply to his question.

He was about to go to the house of study when his wife said to him, "You know, I had a strange dream last night."

"What!" exclaimed the rabbi. "What did you dream?"

"I dreamed that an angel came and knocked on the window above your bed," she replied, "but you were sound asleep, and the angel could not wake you. Then the angel came and knocked at my window, and I opened it and let the angel in. The angel told me that it was the Angel of Dreams, and that it had been sent by Heaven to deliver a message to you, but since it could not wake you, the angel delivered it to me instead."

"What did the angel say?" asked the amazed rabbi.

"It said I could only whisper the message to you." Then she whispered into his ear everything that the angel had revealed.

The next day, the day before Purim, Rabbi Or Shraga summoned all the elders of the congregation. And at midnight, he met with them in the synagogue. "Long ago," he told them, "the Jews of a Persian city were endangered by an evil vizier, whose name was Haman. But Mordecai and Esther defeated him with the help of Heaven.

"We, too, are Persian Jews in grave danger, just as in the time of Mordecai. We know that if the city falls into the hands of the rebels, they will destroy every one of us. Therefore we must put our faith in Heaven, and Heaven has revealed to me that if there is one among us willing to sacrifice his life, then we will be saved."

Now there was a very old rabbi among them who said, "I know that my days are numbered, and I am willing to sacrifice a few days of my life for the sake of the people."

Rabbi Or Shraga and all the elders thanked the old rabbi with all their hearts. Then Rabbi Or Shraga told him, "Before you come to the synagogue in the morning for Purim services, go and immerse yourself seven times in the waters of a *mikvah*. Once you have purified yourself, write on parchment the name of the angel that I will whisper to you, the angel who brings about victory in battle. But know that three hours after you write the angel's name, your spirit will take leave of this world and rise to the Throne of Glory."

The old man accepted this exalted mission, and the next day, when it was Purim, he purified himself, and wrote on a perfect piece of parchment the name that the rabbi had whispered into his ear. He brought it to the synagogue, where all the Jews of the city had gathered to celebrate Purim and to pray that the city be saved, and he gave it to Rabbi Or Shraga.

The rabbi led the frightened congregation in prayer, and then fastened the parchment to the right wing of a white dove. With all those in the synagogue watching and praying for a miracle, the rabbi carried the dove to a window facing east and set it free. As the dove took flight and passed over the heads of the rebels, huge tongues of fire broke out everywhere in the rebel camp. The terrified rebels fled in all directions, never to return. Thus did peace come to the city of Yezd. As for the old man who wrote down the secret name, three hours later he departed from this world and was welcomed into the World to Come.

Every year on Purim after that, the Jews of Yezd not only celebrated the victory of the ancient Persian Jews, but also their own victory, thanks to a miracle of God. So, too, did they fondly remember the old man who had made their victory possible, by giving his life in writing down that holy name.

*Persia, oral tradition*

ABOUT
## "THE ANGEL OF DREAMS"

*Purim*

Purim celebrates the events described in the Biblical Book of Esther. On Purim the *megillah*, the scroll of Esther, is read in the synagogue. The story tells how Haman, the advisor to Ahasuerus, king of Persia, plotted to destroy the Jews of the land. He was stopped by Mordecai and by Esther, the queen, who took great risks and showed great courage in their efforts to save their people.

They ultimately defeated Haman, and it is their triumph that is celebrated on Purim, a joyous holiday with a carnival-like spirit. Children wear costumes and play with special noisemakers known as *graggers*, which are used to drown out Haman's name, and everyone celebrates with special foods, like *hamantashen*, a pastry made in the shape of Haman's hat.

(In present-day Israel they are called *ozney haman*, Haman's ears.) In some communities, the children write Haman's name on the soles of their shoes with chalk, and then stamp out the name. Since Purim is also dedicated to remembering the poor, there is a popular custom called *mishloah manot* in which gifts of food are delivered to the poor and to friends of the family. Sometimes these gifts are sent on special Purim plates containing verses from the Book of Esther.

### *Rabbi Or Shraga*

From at least the ninth century, the Persian city of Yezd was a center for Jewish scholars. Rabbi Or Shraga was the leader of the Jewish community, and he maintained close contact with the Jews of the Persian city of Meshed, another great center of Jewish scholarship. This story demonstrates the close ties between Rabbi Or Shraga and the Shah who ruled the city. In many ways it is parallel to the ancient story of Purim, with Rabbi Or Shraga playing a role similar to that of Mordecai. This demonstrates how events in Jewish history seem to repeat themselves, and how Jewish folklore finds ways to point out these parallels.

## THE MAGIC WINE CUP
### *A Passover Tale*

In the days before Passover, a stranger was seen wandering through the streets of Mogador in the land of Morocco. Even though he was dressed in rags, he did not look like a beggar, and from the fringes on the garment he was wearing it was clear that he was a Jew.

Some of Rabbi Hayim Pinto's students wondered about this man when they saw him in the city market. And when they returned to the yeshivah, they told the rabbi about him. Rabbi Pinto had them describe the man in great detail. Then he asked them if the man had looked happy or sad. They told the rabbi that he had looked terribly sad. Indeed, just looking at his face made them sad as well.

Now, Passover is a time to remember the poor, and it was Rabbi Pinto's custom to invite the poor Jews of the city to his Seder. So on the eve of Passover he sent his students into the city to bring back all the poor Jews they could find. He told them to search especially for the stranger they had told him about, and to be sure that he came back with them.

So the rabbi's students searched every corner of the city for the poor, who were delighted to learn that they would have a place to celebrate the first night of Passover. But when the students finally found the stranger, he was sitting alone under a barren tree, and he refused to accompany them to the rabbi's Seder. "For you it is the holiday of Passover," he said, "but for me it is a time of mourning." The students did their best to persuade him, but in the end they returned empty-handed.

Now, when they told Rabbi Pinto that the man had refused their invitation, the rabbi said, "If you can't convince him to come here, whisper this word in his ear"—and he whispered it to each of his students. So the students returned to the stranger, still sitting under the tree, and they tried once more to invite him to join the rabbi's Seder. Again he refused, but this time one of the students whispered the rabbi's word into the man's ear. And as soon as he heard it, the man's eyes opened wide. He stood up and agreed to accompany them at once.

When that Jew arrived at the rabbi's house, he was greeted warmly by Rabbi Pinto. The man returned the rabbi's greetings, and then he asked, "How is it, Rabbi, that you knew the name of the ship that brought about my misfortune?"

"Join our Seder," Rabbi Pinto replied, "and you will understand how it became known to me. For now, please make yourself at home. I will have a bath prepared for you, and my students will give you fresh clothing."

The man thanked the rabbi, but he was still curious about how he had known his secret.

That night, when everyone was seated at the Seder, Rabbi Pinto introduced the guest and asked him to tell the others his story. This he did. "I was born in the city of Marrakesh," he said, "and I traveled to Spain and worked there until I had become quite wealthy. After several years, I began to miss my native land of Morocco, and thought about returning there to raise a family. With all that I had saved, I bought precious jewels.

"There was a widow whom I befriended. When she learned I was planning to return to Morocco, where her daughter lives, she asked me to bring her daughter her rightful inheritance, jewels that had belonged to her father. I agreed to do so, and I carried everything in a wooden case. But when a storm sank the ship in which I was traveling, the case was lost at sea. Somehow I managed to grab a plank and reached the shores of this city a few weeks ago. I know that I am fortunate to be alive, but after all these years, I have nothing. Even so, that is not what grieves me the most. Above all, I am heartbroken that I cannot fulfill my mission for the widow."

Now, when all those seated at the Seder heard this story, their hearts went out to the poor man who had suffered such a misfortune. Among them, there was one beautiful young woman who had tears flowing down her face. And when the man saw her grief, he, too, broke down and wept.

Rabbi Pinto said, "Do not grieve as we celebrate the Seder, but watch closely." He pointed to the Kiddush cup, which was filled with wine, and pronounced a spell over it. That spell called forth Rahab, the Angel of the Sea.

Just then everyone at the table heard a deep voice say, "Yes, Rabbi Pinto, what is your command?" They trembled with fear, for they could not see where the voice was coming from.

Then the rabbi said, "I call upon you, Rahab, Prince of the Sea, for help in finding what has been lost."

Suddenly, to everyone's amazement, the Kiddush cup began to grow larger and larger, and the wine in it was transformed into the waves of the sea. One after another the waves rose and fell, and eventually they cast up a small wooden case, which floated on the surface. The guest could hardly contain himself. "Master, that is my case!" he cried.

"Take it out!" said Rabbi Pinto. So the man reached into the enormous cup, took out the wooden case and set it on the table. At that instant the cup returned to its original size, and the waters in it became wine once more.

As everyone watched in awe, the man opened the case and saw that nothing was missing. He shed tears of joy. Then Rabbi Pinto said to him, "Now, let me introduce you to the widow's daughter to whom you were delivering the jewels." At that, the young woman who had wept at hearing the man's tale stood up with a radiant smile, and the man almost fainted with surprise. When he had regained his composure, he picked up the wooden case and placed it in her hands, much to the delight of everyone present. Then Rabbi Pinto smiled and said, "Know that nothing happens by accident. All is foretold by the Holy One, blessed be He, as is your meeting here today, for now I can tell you that I heard a heavenly voice announce that you two are destined to wed."

So it was that everyone celebrated that Seder with great happiness, and not long

after, the blessed couple was wed. From then on, every Passover, when they filled the Kiddush cup, they told the story of Rabbi Pinto and the magic wine cup that had changed their lives.

*Syria, oral tradition*

ABOUT
"THE MAGIC WINE CUP"

*Passover*

Passover recalls the liberation of the Israelites from slavery more than three thousand years ago. The Israelites were slaves in Egypt when God commanded Moses to tell the Egyptian Pharaoh to let the people go. When Pharaoh refused, God sent ten plagues. The tenth and most terrible plague killed every firstborn Egyptian male child. The Israelites, who had marked the doorposts of their homes with the blood of a lamb, were spared from this plague when the Angel of Death *passed over* their homes. The name Passover comes from this event. Because the Jews were slaves in Egypt, it is the custom to offer aid to the poor at this time, and to invite the hungry to share in the Seder.

Passover recalls as well the miracle of the parting of the Red Sea (also known as the Sea of Reeds), which permitted the Israelites to escape from the Egyptian army. The festival of Passover begins on the fifteenth day of the Hebrew month of Nisan (in March or April) and lasts for eight days. The highlight of the holiday is the Seder, a family meal with many symbolic foods, held on the first two nights. The Haggadah, a guidebook to the Seder, is read to recall the Exodus from Egypt. During Passover, Jews eat unleavened bread called matzah, to remind them of the unleavened bread that the Israelites made in the wilderness, when there was not time to let their dough rise. Above all, Passover represents the struggle of the Jewish people to be free of any kind of bondage.

### Rabbi Hayim Pinto

Rabbi Hayim Pinto (who lived in the first half of the nineteenth century) is one of the most famous of the Moroccan rabbis. He lived in the city of Mogador most of his life. He belonged to an illustrious family, which included his father, son, and grandson all renowned for Torah study. He died at a ripe old age in 1845. His descendants now live in Ashdod, Israel.

During his lifetime, he was known for his vast knowledge and the miracles he is said to have accomplished. In this story, Rabbi Hayim Pinto shows himself to be a great kabbalistic conjurer.

## THE DREAM OF THE RABBI'S DAUGHTER
### *A Lag ba-Omer Tale*

Safed is a city in the north of Israel that has been the home of many mystics, where many a miracle has been known to take place. This is one such story.

There once was a young girl named Zohara, who had a great love of learning. Her father, Rabbi Gedalya, had named her after his favorite book, the Zohar, the most important book of Jewish mysticism. He taught her how to read Hebrew so she could join in the prayers with her mother. But he did not teach her Aramaic, the language in which the Zohar was written.

In those days it was the custom in Safed for all the leading rabbis to go to the village of Meron on the holiday of Lag ba-Omer to pray at the tomb of Rabbi Shimon bar Yohai. The families of the rabbis sometimes accompanied them to Meron, and there they set up tents outside the tomb. So it was that Zohara accompanied her father on the journey.

Now, there are two entrances to the shrine built around the tomb, one for men and the other for women, each entrance leading to a different chamber. On the men's side, the rabbis sat in a circle and passed around the mystical book of the Zohar, which Rabbi Shimon bar Yohai was said to have written. Each of the rabbis read a passage from the book; then they discussed its meaning.

Meanwhile, Zohara was on the women's side, where the women were quietly praying. She could hear all that the rabbis said in the other part of the shrine, although she could not see them. She stayed there for a long time, even after the other women finished praying and returned to their tents. She tried to follow the rabbis' discussion, but she could not, since the Zohar was written in Aramaic.

As Zohara struggled to understand the words of the rabbis, she became very sad and began to weep. She wanted so much to understand what they were saying! She wept a long time, until she became so tired that she fell asleep.

While Zohara slept, she dreamed that she was in a cave lit by a bonfire, where a rabbi with a long, white beard was teaching a class. In the dream Zohara looked around and recognized all of the greatest sages of Safed, including her father, who was sitting next to her, listening closely as the teacher spoke.

Finally the old teacher asked his students a question, but none of them knew the answer. All at once, he looked right at Zohara and asked her if she knew. Zohara was very surprised that he had called on her, and she remained silent, for she was ashamed that she did not even understand the question, much less know the answer. Then the old rabbi told her to stand up, and when she did, he blessed her with a great blessing and said, "Know that your soul is a precious one, Zohara, a soul that has come down from the highest Heaven. Know, too, that when your father named you Zohara, he bound us together. You will never have to be sad again because you do not understand. After this, whenever anyone repeats the words of the Zohar, I will come to you, and you will understand better than the best."

That is when Zohara woke up. From where she sat, she could still hear the rabbis on the other side of the wall discussing the Zohar. But this time, Zohara was astonished to discover that she understood everything they said. Then the rabbis reached such a difficult passage that none of them knew what it meant. They tried to interpret it for a long time, but at last they gave up and returned to their tents.

Zohara also left the shrine and returned to her family's tent. She told her father that she had overheard their discussion. When she repeated the difficult passage word for word, her father was amazed. "How is it possible that you can repeat these words, when you cannot even understand the language in which they are written?" he said.

Zohara then proceeded to tell her father exactly what the words meant and to explain the problem that had baffled the rabbis. Hearing his young daughter speak with such remarkable wisdom, he was filled with wonder.

Zohara told him of her dream, and of how the old rabbi had blessed her, and how he had promised to come to her whenever she heard the words of the Zohar. Her father was astounded. "I know who that old rabbi must have been," he told her.

"Please, father, who was he?" she asked.

"Surely," said Rabbi Gedalya, "he was none other than Rabbi Shimon bar Yohai himself, who came to you on Lag ba-Omer, the day in which we recall his life and death. For know that Shimon bar Yohai lived in a cave for thirteen years, and that we light campfires on Lag ba-Omer in his honor. That must be the meaning of the cave in your dream, and of the bonfire you saw burning there. Surely this means that Shimon bar Yohai has chosen to speak through you."

Rabbi Gedalya told the other rabbis about his daughter's dream and how the wisdom of Shimon bar Yohai fell from her lips. They found it hard to believe that such a miracle had taken place, and they asked if they could see for themselves.

So the rabbis of Safed came to Rabbi Gedalya's home and questioned Zohara about the most difficult passages in the Zohar. Every time she replied without hesitation, with answers so clear the rabbis felt foolish for not having understood in the first place.

Every time Zohara heard the words of the Zohar, the rabbi's spirit returned to her, revealing any mystery she wanted to know. Forever after, the rabbis of Safed treated Zohara with the greatest respect and sought her help in understanding the Zohar, for they knew that she spoke with the wisdom of Shimon bar Yohai.

*Israel, oral tradition*

ABOUT
## "THE DREAM OF THE RABBI'S DAUGHTER"

*Lag ba-Omer*

In the days of Rabbi Akiba, who lived in the first century C.E., there was a terrible plague that killed many thousands of his students. The day that the plague finally ended, the eighteenth day of Iyyar (in May), was declared a holiday, known as Lag ba-Omer, which means the thirty-third day of counting the Omer. The Omer is a sheaf of barley from the new grain harvest that was brought to the Holy Temple as an offering on the second day of Passover. The Torah commands the people to count seven weeks from the time of offering the Omer ending on the holiday of Shavuot.

In later times, Lag ba-Omer also became linked with the day manna first began to fall, which is described in chapter 16 of Exodus. But at present this holiday is more strongly associated with Rabbi Shimon bar Yohai, who was said to have spent thirteen years hiding in a cave from the Romans, finally emerging on the day of Lag ba-Omer.

Lag ba-Omer is a popular holiday in modern Israel, in which campfires are lit all over the country, but especially in the Galilee, in honor of Shimon bar Yohai. Huge crowds gather at his tomb for a joyous celebration, and scores of weddings are held, adding to the festive atmosphere. Lag ba-Omer is also a day on which the book of the Zohar is studied, as in this tale.

### Rabbi Shimon bar Yohai

Rabbi Shimon bar Yohai, one of the great talmudic sages, lived in the second century C.E. He was a pupil of Rabbi Akiba. At that time the Romans had conquered Jerusalem and had forbidden the study of the Torah. Rabbi Shimon criticized the Romans privately, but a traitor reported his comments to the Romans, who condemned him to death.

So Rabbi Shimon and his son Elazar went into hiding in a cave near the city of Tiberias for thirteen years. Legend has it that a spring miraculously appeared in that cave to provide them with fresh water, and a carob tree grew outside the cave to hide them and provide them with food.

Elijah the Prophet is also said to have visited them every day and taught them secrets of Heaven. Tradition holds that Rabbi Shimon wrote down these secrets, which formed the famous book of the Zohar, the primary text of Jewish mysticism. However, modern scholars say that the Zohar was not written by Shimon bar Yohai in the second century, but by Rabbi Moshe de Leon in the thirteenth century. Shimon bar Yohai's grave is found in Meron in northern Israel, and a shrine has been built around it, exactly as described in this story.

## Spirit Possession in Judaism

Jewish folklore describes two kinds of possession by spirits. The most famous kind is known as possession by a *dybbuk*. A *dybbuk* is the spirit of a dead person, usually an evil one, that enters the body of a vulnerable person and takes possession of him or her. An exorcism ceremony must be done in order to expel the evil spirit. An example of *dybbuk* possession is found in the famous play *The Dybbuk*, by S. Ansky, first performed in 1920. Here a bride is possessed by the *dybbuk* on the day of her wedding, and the final act of the play presents an authentic rabbinic exorcism ceremony.

There is another kind of possession in Jewish tradition, a positive kind. This is known as possession by *ibbur* (literally, "impregnation.") An *ibbur* is the spirit of a dead sage who comes back to aid someone. The *ibbur* fuses with the soul of the person it is helping, instilling additional faith and wisdom. Unlike a *dybbuk*, which must be exorcised, an *ibbur* usually possesses someone only temporarily and is associated with some kind of sacred object, such as the book of the Zohar in this story.

## A GIFT FOR JERUSALEM
### *A Shavuot Tale*

Long ago, in the hills of the Galilee, far from the city of Jerusalem, there lived a boy named Haninah ben Dosa, who was the son of a stonecutter. Haninah came from a poor family. They were so poor that they had little to eat except for the carobs and olives that grew wild.

Every year, before Shavuot, the people of Hanina's village would prepare to go up to Jerusalem for an annual pilgrimage to the Holy Temple. They would take the finest fruits of the harvest, or the finest sheep or goat from their herds, bringing them as a gift for the Temple.

Haninah would watch his neighbors as they prepared for their journey. He listened carefully as they told tales of past visits to Jerusalem; they spoke of the cool, crisp air there, of the beautiful sunsets, and of the magnificent Holy Temple, shining with gold. Haninah heard their stories and wished to go to Jerusalem more than anything. But Haninah's family was so poor that they had neither an animal nor any fruits to offer. So it was that year after year, Haninah watched his neighbors as they left for their journey, returning with tales of the golden city of Jerusalem.

Haninah would help his friends and neighbors pack and prepare for their journey. But one year, Haninah was so sad that he wouldn't be able to go that he took a walk instead. He walked through the village, his head bowed down.

Suddenly, he came across a stone. It was the biggest stone he had ever seen, and Haninah came up with a wonderful idea. He ran home, hurrying past his neighbors.

He grabbed a hammer and a chisel, and ran back to the site of the stone.

Then Haninah started to work on that stone. He chiseled and fashioned it, carving in beautiful designs. The next day, he ran back to the stone and continued his work. For three days, Haninah worked on the stone, taking breaks only for meals. Finally he polished the stone until it shone brightly in the sun.

Haninah stepped back and looked at his finished stone, smiling widely. He had carved four majestic angels. "This," he exclaimed triumphantly, "is the best thing I have ever made. It will be perfect for the Temple in Jerusalem."

Haninah ran to invite his neighbors to see his work of art. They gathered around the stone.

"Haninah, this is truly a masterpiece!" said the baker.

"Look at the detail of the wings. The angels appear so alive," said the weaver.

"Yes, as if they could jump out of the stone and fly," added the shoemaker.

"Oh," said Haninah, "then you can take it with you on your journey to Jerusalem! For if I can't go to Jerusalem, at least my gift will go." Haninah put his arms around that stone and tried to lift it, to give it to them. But the stone did not budge. He tried again. Nothing.

The neighbors looked at each other baffled. Their eyes turned downward, they replied: "Haninah, the stone is beautiful. But it is much too heavy for us to take on the long journey to Jerusalem. Maybe you can draw a picture of the angels and we could take that instead." Haninah did not utter a word. One by one, the neighbors went back to their preparations. When they had all gone, Haninah stretched out on his rock and cried.

Now God looked down from Heaven and saw Haninah's deep desire to go to Jerusalem. God saw the love and dedication he had put into creating a gift for the Temple. And God caused a miracle to take place. As Haninah's tears rolled across that stone, each tear touched one of the stone angels, and at that instant they rose up and came to life, much to Haninah's amazement.

Then, with a swift flap of their wings, the four angels lifted the stone, with Haninah on top of it, up into the air. Haninah found himself flying across the heav-

ens toward Jerusalem, along with the angels. As they approached Jerusalem, the city first appeared as a jewel glowing in the distance. Haninah laughed out loud. "Now I know why Jerusalem is called the jewel in God's crown!"

Soon Haninah was standing near the entrance of the Temple in Jerusalem, and the stone rested beside him, with the angels carved into the stone once more. Just then a group of weary pilgrims arrived, and when they saw what Haninah had carved, they said, "Look at that beautiful stone! Let us rest here." Haninah was filled with joy, for a miracle had brought his gift to Jerusalem, and now it would serve as a place for weary travelers to sit and rest.

When Haninah ben Dosa grew up, he became one of the greatest rabbis. Even to this day, people tell loving tales about him. As for the stone he had carved, it remained there as long as the Temple was still standing. But when the Temple was torn down, the stone disappeared. Some say it was used in rebuilding the walls of Jerusalem. Others say that the same angels who brought it to Jerusalem later brought it to the magical Temple in heavenly Jerusalem, where Haninah now makes his home.

*Babylon, fifth century*

ABOUT
"A GIFT FOR JERUSALEM"

*Shavuot*

Shavuot takes place on the sixth day of the Hebrew month of Sivan (in May or June). It was originally a spring harvest festival in the land of Israel, one of three yearly pilgrimage festivals in Judaism, along with Passover and Sukkot. All three festivals recall the events of the Exodus from Egypt. While Passover celebrates the departure from Egypt, and Sukkot commemorates the forty years the Israelites wandered in the desert, Shavuot celebrates the day on which the Ten Commandments and the rest of the Torah were given at Mount Sinai, establishing an eternal covenant between God and the Jewish people.

It was the custom in ancient Israel for all of the people to gather at the Temple in Jerusalem during the three pilgrimage festivals. They would bring an offering for the Temple—as Haninah does in this story—usually the best of their harvest or livestock. In this way they gave their thanks to God. Haninah's gift is an unusual one in that it does not fit into either of these categories.

In the Sephardic prayerbook, a Jewish wedding contract (a *ketubah*) is read on Shavuot, in which God is described as the bridegroom and Israel as the bride, and they swear eternal allegiance to each other. Thus celebrating Shavuot reenacts the ancient covenant of the Jewish people with God.

### Rabbi Haninah ben Dosa

Haninah ben Dosa, who lived in the first century C.E., grew up to become one of the most respected and beloved of the talmudic rabbis. He lived in the Land of Israel in the town of Arav in the Galilee, where he worked as a stonecutter. Although he and his wife were extremely poor, Rabbi Hanina refused to accept charity, and often all they had to eat were carob pods.

The miracle that takes place in this story shows that God cares not about the gift itself but the intention in giving it. That is why angels appear to help Haninah carry the heavy stone all the way to Jerusalem.

It is said that Rabbi Haninah was so righteous that God showed favor to the entire generation for his sake.

### *Ascending to Jerusalem (Aliyah)*

Jerusalem is in the hills of Israel, and those who go there are said to *ascend* to Jerusalem. The Hebrew term for this is *aliyah,* which means "ascent." This term is also used in the synagogue for those who are called upon to "ascend" to the pulpit, to participate in the reading of the Torah. Jews living outside of Israel who decide to move there are said to "go up to the Land of Israel." The modern term is to "make *aliyah.*" Thus the use of the term *"aliyah"* in connection with Jerusalem shows just how holy the city is considered to be.

## THE DAY THE RABBI DISAPPEARED
### *A Sabbath Tale*

The sages of Fez had a dream: to bring the greatest living sage in the world to visit their city in the land of Morocco. It is said that for every two Jews, you will find three opinions, but in this matter all agreed: the greatest sage was none other than Moses Maimonides, known to the world as the Rambam.

At that time, the Rambam was living in Egypt. But before he had written his great books and had become the Jewish leader of the city of Cairo, he had lived in Fez for several years. Now his illustrious name was spoken of wherever Jews could be found, and the sages of Fez longed to study Torah with him again. So they sent a messenger to Cairo, inviting him to return for a visit. And before a month had passed, the messenger brought back a letter from the Rambam.

The sages were delighted to learn that the Rambam would indeed be coming to Fez. But they were mystified, too. For the Rambam had written that although he would stay in Fez for a month, he would spend each Sabbath in the city of Jerusalem. How was that possible? Jerusalem was far away, and if the Rambam spent the week in Fez, he could never reach Jerusalem by the Sabbath.

One of the sages spoke. "Perhaps the Rambam does not want us to interpret his words literally. Perhaps he means to say that on the Sabbath his heart lies in Jerusalem, so much so that it is as if he were not present among us." The others marveled at the wisdom of these words.

At last the Rambam arrived. He was greeted with joy by the entire Jewish population of Fez. Each day he met with the sages, sharing his knowledge of the Torah. But on Friday the Rambam asked to remain alone, so that he could prepare for the Sabbath. And at sunset, when the Sabbath began, the Rambam was nowhere to be seen. The people understood that he must have gone somewhere else. But where? For there was simply no way he could have reached Jerusalem.

Then, right after the Havdalah ceremony that ends the Sabbath, the Rambam rejoined the sages, and when they asked him where he had been, he said, "In Jerusalem."

This happened two more times. Every week, just before the beginning of the Sabbath, the Rambam disappeared. And no one knew where he went.

Now there were two boys in Fez who had heard tales of the Rambam's miracles. They believed him when he said he went to Jerusalem on the Sabbath, and more than anything in the world, they wanted to know how he did it. So they climbed a tree outside his house and waited and watched.

The Rambam spent all day Friday writing in his study, until a few minutes before sunset. Then he went up the stairs to the roof, wearing his Sabbath robe.

The boys could see the Rambam clearly from the tree, but he didn't seem to notice them. His gaze was turned inward. Then, just before sunset heralded the onset of the Sabbath, he pronounced a spell consisting of strange names the boys had never heard. All at once they saw something like a falling star that landed right where the Rambam was standing, and then it was gone. And they saw that the Rambam, too, had disappeared.

The boys could hardly believe their eyes, yet they had seen the miracle themselves. They decided that the Rambam must have pronounced a magic spell invoking an angel—for what else could that falling star have been?—and now surely, he was praying in Jerusalem.

And they were right.

*Morocco, oral tradition*

ABOUT

## "THE DAY THE RABBI DISAPPEARED"

### The Sabbath

The Book of Genesis tells how God created the world in six days and rested on the seventh, making it a holy day, the Sabbath. Every week Jews observe the Sabbath as a day of joy and rest. The famous Jewish philosopher Ahad Ha'am once said, "More than Israel has kept the Sabbath, the Sabbath has kept Israel." This means that the existence of the Sabbath has given a special rhythm and meaning to Jewish life. The commandment to keep the Sabbath is the fourth of the ten commandments: *Remember the Sabbath day to keep it holy. Six days you shall labor and do all your work, but the seventh day is a sabbath of God: you shall not do any work* (Exodus 20:8–10).

The Sabbath is very much a family holiday and a time to appreciate things at a leisurely pace. Sabbath rituals include Friday evening services, where a special prayer, *Lekhah Dodi*, is sung to welcome the Sabbath Queen. At home there is the lighting of the Sabbath candles and a family Sabbath meal, with blessings over wine and bread. There is an ancient tradition that every Jew receives a second soul during the Sabbath, known as a *neshamah yetayrah*. A special ceremony for the end of the Sabbath, known as Havdalah, includes the smelling of fragrant spices that symbolize reluctance to see the Sabbath end—and one's second soul depart.

### The Rambam

Rabbi Moses ben Maimon (1135–1204) is known both as Maimonides and by the Hebrew acronym Rambam. As the greatest Jewish philosopher, he is so highly regarded that the inscription on his tombstone reads, "From Moses [in the Bible] to Moses [Maimonides], there was none like Moses." The Rambam lived most of his life in Egypt, where he was the court physician as well as the leader of the Jewish community. He did, however, live in the city of Fez for several years, as reported in this tale, which was collected in modern Israel from a Jew from the city of Fez.

Among the Rambam's most famous books are the *Mishneh Torah*, a commentary on the Mishnah, and *The Guide to the Perplexed*. The Rambam defined the "Thirteen Principles of Faith," which became the essential list of Jewish beliefs. Although he himself disputed the existence of magic, there are many legends about him found throughout the Middle East in which he plays the role of a sorcerer, as in this tale.

# GLOSSARY

**etrog** (EH-troge) A citrus fruit, the citron, that is carried and shaken with the *lulav* during the Sukkot synagogue service.

*Gan Eden* (GAHN AY-den) The Garden of Eden.

*gragger* (GRAH-ger) Noisemaker used to celebrate Purim.

**hamantashen** (HAH-mun-tah-shun) Three-cornered pastries served on Purim, said to have been modeled on Haman's hat.

*hanukkiyah* (hah-nu-key-YAH) A special eight-branched menorah with a *shammash*, a helper candle, used during the eight days of Hanukkah.

**Hasidism** (ha-SEED-ism or ha-seed-IS-um) A movement of spiritual revival in Judaism founded by the Baal Shem Tov in the eighteenth century. It emphasizes ways of becoming closer to God through prayer, dancing, singing, and storytelling.

*hazan* (hah-ZAHN or HAH-zun) A cantor.

**Hoshanah Rabbah** (ho-SHAH-nah RAH-bah) The seventh and final day of Sukkot, on which it is customary to stay up studying all night. Legend holds that the heavens open for an instant at midnight, and any wish made at that time comes true.

**Kabbalah** (literally "to receive"; kah-bah-LA or kah-BAH-la) The Jewish mystical tradition and its literature.

**Kiddush cup** (key-DOOSH or KID-dish) A goblet used when blessings are said over wine on the Sabbath and other holidays.

**lulav** (loo-LAHV or LOO-lahv) A palm branch, tied together with sprigs of willow and myrtle, carried and shaken during the Sukkot synagogue service.

**Megillah** (literally "scroll"; meh-gi-LA or meh-GIL-la) Usually refers to the Book of Esther.

**menorah** (meh-no-RA or men-NO-ra) The seven-branched candelabrum described in the Bible and used in Temple days.

**mikvah** (MIK-vah) The pool used for ritual purification, primarily by women.

**minyan** (min-YAHN or MIN-yahn) A prayer service traditionally requires a minimum of ten men in order to take place. These ten men are known as a *minyan*. Many congregations now count women in the *minyan* as well.

**Rabbi** A teacher of Judaism who is qualified to decide matters of Jewish law.

**Seder** (SAY-der) A ritual meal that takes place during Passover.

*shalom aleichem* (literally "Peace unto you"; sha-LOME ah-LAY-hem) The traditional Jewish greeting. The reply is *Aleichem shalom,* meaning "Unto you, peace."

**shofar** (sho-FAR or SHO-fur) A ram's horn, used as a wind instrument.

**Talmud** (tal-MOOD or TAL-mud) The second most sacred Jewish text, after the Torah. The Talmud was codified around the fifth century C.E.

**Tetragrammaton** (te-truh-GRA-muh-ton) A Greek word for the four-letter name of God, whose true pronunciation is a great secret. Jews substitute *Adonai* or *Ha-Shem* when they reach this word in their prayers.

**Torah** (toe-RAH or TOE-rah) The first five books of the Bible, which God is said to have dictated to Moses at Mount Sinai. The most sacred Jewish text of all.

**yeshivah** (yuh-SHE-vah) A school for Jewish students, in which they are taught primarily Torah and Talmud.

**Zohar** (ZO-har) The central work of Jewish mysticism, traditionally attributed to Rabbi Shimon bar Yohai of the second century C.E. but now considered to have been written in the thirteenth century by Rabbi Moshe de Leon and his disciples.

# SOURCES

All sources are in Hebrew unless otherwise noted.

*A Flock of Angels* (**Kurdistan**) From *Kehillot Yehudei Kurdistan*, edited by Abraham Ben-Jacob (Jerusalem, 1961). A variant is IFA (Israel Folktale Archives) 11165, collected by Avraham Keren from Yitzak Izador Firestein of Poland.

*Drawing the Wind* (**The Balkans**) This story was collected during World War I by the folklorist Max Grunwald from an unknown Jewish teller from the Balkans. It was published in *Sippurei-am, Romanssot, ve-Orehot-hayim shel Yehude Sefarad* by Max Grunwald, edited by Dov Noy (Jerusalem, 1982). There are many variants of this tale told among Sephardic communities. The Israel Folktale Archives has collected more than one hundred versions. In some versions the imprisoned rabbi is identified as Rabbi Ephraim ben Yisrael Ankawa of Tlemcen, Tunisia.

*The Cottage of Candles* (**Afghanistan**) IFA 7830, collected by Zevulon Qort from Ben Zion Asherov, published in *Sippurei-am Mipi Yehudei Afghanistan* (Tel Aviv, 1983). A variant is found in *Ha-Na'al ha-Ktanah*, edited by Asher Barash (Tel Aviv, 1966). Another variant, in which there are bottles of oil in a cave, and a person lives until the oil is exhausted is IFA 8335, collected by Moshe Rabi from Hannah Haddad, in *Avotenu Sipru* (Jerusalem, 1976). "Godfather Death" is a variant of this story found in *Grimm's Fairy Tales*.

*Four Who Entered Paradise* (**Morocco**) IFA 13901, collected by Yaakov Alfasi of Morocco from Rabbi Shimon Elkayam of Azmor, Morocco. This tale is clearly based on the famous tale about four sages who entered Paradise found in the Babylonian Talmud (Haggigah 14b). Traditions about Hoshanah Rabbah are from IFA 1257, collected by Zevulun Qort from Zohara Bezalel of Afghanistan. A variant about the sky opening (this time on Shavuot) is IFA 4014, collected by Pinhas Gutterman from Rabbi Shalom Weinstein of Poland.

*The Flying Shoe* (**Eastern Europe**) From *Gan ha-Hasidut*, edited by Eliezer Steinmann (Jerusalem, 1957).

*The Enchanted Menorah* (**Germany**) From *Me-Otsar Genazai* by Hayim Dov Armon Kastenbaum, edited by Alter Ze'ev Wortheim (Tel Aviv, 1932). From Hayim Dov Armon Kastenbaum, who heard this story from his grandmother.

*The Souls of Trees* (**Eastern Europe**) From *Sihot Moharan* in *Hayye Moharan* by Rabbi Nathan of Bratslav (Lemberg, West Ukraine, 1874). Rabbi Nathan was Rabbi Nachman's scribe, and wrote down all his teachings. The passage Rabbi Nachman's finger lands on is from the Talmud (B. Baba Kama 92b and B. Sukkah 29a).

*The Angel of Dreams* (**Persia**) IFA 1375. Collected by Hanina Mizrahi from Yaakov Yazdi.

*The Magic Wine Cup* (**Syria**) IFA 6628, collected by Moshe Rabi from Avraham Etia, in *Avotenu Sipru*, edited by Moshe Rabi (Jerusalem, 1976), story no. 47.

*The Dream of the Rabbi's Daughter* (**Israel**) IFA 612, collected by S. Arnest.

*A Gift for Jerusalem* (**Babylon**) From the Babylonian Talmud (Taanit 25a). An oral variant is IFA 399 from Poland.

*The Day the Rabbi Disappeared* (**Morocco**) IFA 15512. Collected by Yifrach Haviv from Yoram Harush of Fez, Morocco.